ISBN 978-1-952425-00-4 (Paperback Edition)
ISBN 978-1-952425-02-8 (Hardcover Edition)

All rights reserved. Published by Jackal Moon Press.
Lexington, Kentucky.

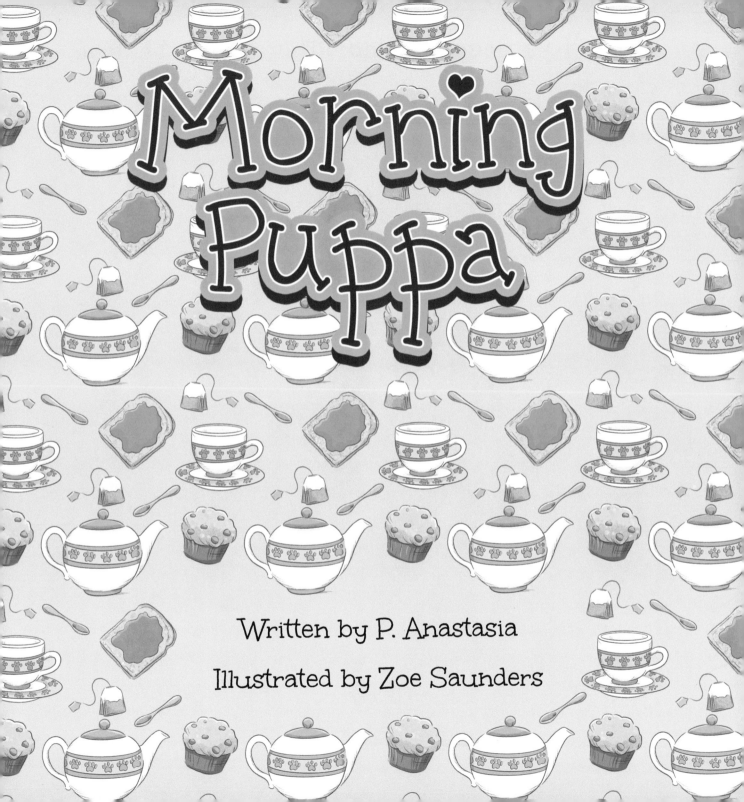

Morning Puppa

Written by P. Anastasia

Illustrated by Zoe Saunders

Help! I've been burgled! This cannot be true.

My teacup is missing! Oh, what should I do?

No black, white, or green. No oolong for me!
Without my cup, how can I have tea?

It was safe by my bed
when I went to sleep.

Was porcelain plundered
as I counted sheep?

I'll fetch my friend, Matcha,
and we'll catch the crook.

He's not where I left him.
I've searched every nook.

Earl could solve this curious plot...

If he were not gone from his usual spot.

Minty and Rose may give me a clue...

Where could they be? Are they missing, too?

I need a snack for my rumbling belly...

I could butter toast, but where is the jelly?

No bread on the counter.

Whoever has done this needs to be caught!

Not a morsel to spare. Not a single tea leaf.

They took it all, that terrible thief!

I give up! I'm done! Right here I will stay.

This doggone mess has ruined my day.

I'm hungry. I'm thirsty.
This morning's been awful!

I need a hot cuppa, a muffin, a waffle...

Biscuits and scones?

Delectable sweets?

Crumpets and cakes? Flapjacks in a stack?

My nose leads the way. I am on the right track.

All of my pals were here
the whole time!

Nothing was stolen.
There was no crime.

A party awaits with
a seat just for me.

Breakfast with friends
is my cup of tea!

Meet Puppa

His friends call him Benjamin.
He's a lovable Australian Shepherd,
and the inspiration behind Morning Puppa.

On sunny days, while his mom sips a hot cup
of her favorite tea, Benjamin frolics through the
meadow and plays in the dirt. Birds flap and chirp
as he shows off his acrobatics.

The only season Benjamin loves more than Spring

is Winter. Snow days are his favorite!

What's your
favorite season?

CPSIA information can be obtained
at www.ICGtesting.com
Printed in the USA
LVHW021310231021
701149LV00003B/31